In the Frog Bog

Written by Margaret Ryan

Illustrated by Benedetta Capriotti

Collins

Down in the farmyard, the frogs sing cheep, but ...

Little Frog barks gruff.

The farmyard frogs yell,
"Stop that racket!"

So Little Frog lands in a garden.

SPLAT!

Deep in the weeds, the garden frogs sing peep.

Little Frog sighs and barks gruff.

The garden frogs ask, "Are you a frog or a dog?"

So Little Frog hops to a bog.

PLOP!

9

High on the sandbank, the boatyard frogs sing cheep, peep, beep.

Sad Little Frog barks gruff and turns to go.

"Join us, Little Frog. We like that song!"

They all jump, thump and sing.

15

After reading

Letters and Sounds: Phase 4

Word count: 107

Focus on adjacent consonants with short vowel phonemes

Common exception words: to, the, go, all, are, we, you, they, like, so, little, ask

Curriculum links (EYFS): Personal, social and emotional development: Making relationships

Curriculum links (National Curriculum, Year 1): PSHE

Early learning goals: Listening and attention: children listen to stories, accurately anticipating key events and respond to what they hear with relevant comments, questions or actions; Understanding: answer 'how' and 'why' questions about their experiences and in response to stories or events; Reading: read and understand simple sentences, use phonic knowledge to decode regular words, read some common irregular words

National Curriculum learning objectives: Spoken language: listen and respond appropriately to adults and their peers; Reading/word reading: apply phonic knowledge and skills as the route to decoding words, read aloud accurately books that are consistent with their developing phonic knowledge; Reading/comprehension: develop pleasure in reading, by being encouraged to link what they read or hear read to their own experiences

Developing fluency

- Your child may enjoy hearing you read the book. Model reading the dialogue with expression.
- You may wish to read alternate pages, encouraging your child to read any dialogue and sound words with expression.

Phonic practice

- Practise reading words that contain adjacent consonants. Model sounding out the following word, saying each of the sounds quickly and clearly. Then blend the sounds together.
  b/u/m/p
- Draw attention to the two consonants at the end of the word, **bump**. Ask your child to find two words that rhyme with **bump** on page 13. (*jump, thump*). Ask them to sound them out and blend them.
- Can your child think of any other words that rhyme with **bump**? (e.g. *grump, lump*)

Extending vocabulary

- Read page 4 to your child. Can they think of another word that could be used instead of **yell**? (e.g. *shout, screech*)
- Can they think of another word that could be used instead of **racket**? (e.g. *noise, din*)

Enid Blyton's

NODDY

Finds a Furry Tail

BBC CHILDREN'S BOOKS

Noddy was in a rush. The night before, he had been to a party at the Noah's Ark with lots of other toys and he had woken up late.

"You are lucky, little car," said Noddy as he hurried out of his house, hastily tying his scarf. "You don't have to get dressed every day."

Noddy was just about to get into his car when he noticed something odd.

"My word, car!" he exclaimed. "There's a furry brown tail on your passenger seat."

Noddy looked at the tail. "It must belong to one of the toys I gave a ride to last night," he said. "I can't remember which one."

The tail felt lovely and soft against Noddy's cheek. "I wonder what I would look like with a tail," he said. He hurried inside to try it on.

Noddy pinned the tail on and admired himself in the mirror.

"I look very, very nice with a tail," he told himself. "I look like a long-tailed Noddy!"

Just then, Mr Tubby Bear popped his head round the door. He looked pleased to see Noddy.

"Can you help me?" asked Mr Tubby Bear. "After the party last night, I'm afraid I woke up late. Will you drive me to the station so that I don't miss my train?"

"Yes, of course," said Noddy.

"Splendid!" said Mr Tubby Bear.

Tessie Bear and Bumpy Dog were out for a walk when Noddy and Mr Tubby Bear drove past in the car. Tessie Bear waved at them.

Noddy was driving so fast that he didn't notice his scarf gradually unwind itself from round his neck.

Only Tessie Bear and Bumpy Dog saw it
blow right off and land on the road.
   "I say, Noddy!" called out Tessie Bear,
but Noddy was already a long way off.

9

Bumpy Dog ran and picked the scarf up and brought it back to Tessie Bear. He barked and barked.

"All right, Bumpy Dog," said Tessie Bear. "You can wear it if you're a good dog. Run after Noddy and give the scarf back to him."

At the railway station Mr Tubby Bear was just in time for his train.

"May I have a return ticket, please," he said to the train driver.

Suddenly, all the toys sitting on the train burst out laughing. "My, oh my!" said Mr Jumbo. "Just look at Noddy!"

"What's the matter?" asked Noddy in surprise.
"Why is everybody laughing?"

He tried to turn round to see what they were all looking at.

"Now then, what's all this laughing about?" asked Mr Plod.

"Look at Noddy's furry tail," sniggered Clockwork Mouse, as the train moved off.

"Goodness gracious, young Noddy," said Mr Plod, trying not to laugh himself. "When did you grow that tail?"

"I didn't grow it," said Noddy. "I found it in my car. I don't know whose tail it is."

"Well, you must find out and return it forthwith!" said Mr
Plod. "Pilfering another toy's tail is a very serious offence."

"What is pilfering?" asked Noddy.

"Pilfering, young Noddy, is stealing," said Mr Plod. "Give
that tail back straight away or I shall be forced to arrest you
as a thief!"

Noddy was feeling very sorry for himself when Bumpy Dog came bounding up and knocked him over.

"You silly Bumpy Dog," said Noddy. "What are you doing?"

Then Noddy noticed that Bumpy Dog was wearing his scarf.

"You must have pilfered my scarf," said Noddy, crossly.
"You're very, very naughty. You are a thief!"

Poor Bumpy Dog looked upset.

"I'm going to return this tail which I *did not* pilfer," said
Noddy, striding off.

Noddy's first idea was that it might be Bert Monkey's tail. Bert Monkey was at the café having an ice-cream. His tail was trying to take Dinah Doll's ice-cream, too.

"Ow!" cried Bert Monkey, as Dinah Doll smacked his tail with her spoon.

"Bert Monkey!" called Noddy, coming up. "Have you lost your tail?"

"I can't have lost it, Noddy," replied Bert Monkey. "It's just started to hurt."

"I didn't really think this could be your tail. It's so soft and furry. Not at all naughty," smiled Noddy.

Then Noddy decided he'd try the Noah's Ark.

"Hello, animals!" cried Noddy, cheerfully. The animals just yawned sleepily. Noddy noticed that they all had their tails. The only animal he couldn't see was Mr Lion. Noddy thought it might be *his* tail.

Mr Lion came to the window of the
ark to look at Noddy's furry tail.
"That's not mine!" he said in
disgust. "It's a silly, furry tail! I have a
long, strong tail." He showed his own
tail to Noddy through the window.

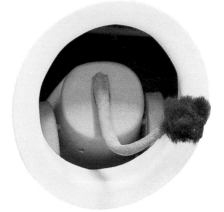

Noddy was on the point of giving up when Mrs Noah came out of the Ark.

"Ah, Noddy! You clever fellow. You've found it," she said, pointing at the furry tail.

"But Mrs Noah," said Noddy in surprise, "*you* haven't got a tail."

"This isn't a tail. This is my new furry scarf," said Mrs Noah. "It's not *real* fur like a tail would be."

"Oh, I am pleased," said Noddy. "Now Mr Plod will have to believe I didn't pilfer it."

Just then, along came Tessie Bear and Bumpy Dog.

"Look!" said Mrs Noah. "Noddy has found the furry scarf I lost."

"Well, how odd!" said Tessie Bear. "Noddy lost his own scarf this morning and Bumpy Dog chased after him to give it back."

"Oh, dear," said Noddy, stroking Bumpy Dog guiltily. "I was so cross with him. I thought he had pilfered it."

Bumpy Dog whined sadly.

"Please cheer up, Bumpy," said Noddy. "I didn't mean to make you miserable."

"Bumpy Dog is so miserable that his tail has lost its wag," said Tessie Bear. "Well, I'm going to look all over Toyland until I find it," declared Noddy.

26

Noddy went up to the zebras. "Excuse me, animals,"
he said. "Have you seen a wag lying about?"
　　But the zebras just yawned.

"Now, wait a minute," said Mrs Noah, sensibly. "All Bumpy Dog needs is a bit of cheering up. Then you'll find his wag comes back all on its own."

Bumpy Dog liked the sound of that.

"Let me think what nice things I've got to eat," said Mrs Noah. "I've got some ginger biscuits, some chocolate cake, some ice-cream – and even a beautiful bone."

Bumpy Dog suddenly looked very cheerful again and his tail started to wag!

Bumpy Dog went leaping up to Noddy and knocked him over.

"I don't know where your wag went to, Bumpy, but it's come back now," said Noddy, laughing.

"It must be fun to wag a tail," said Noddy, as Bumpy Dog licked his face, "but I don't want one after all. Tails cause too much trouble and they take an awful lot of looking after!"

"Woof! Woof!" said Bumpy Dog.

Other Noddy *TV Tie-in titles available from BBC Children's Books:*

Noddy and the Alarm Clock

Noddy Borrows an Umbrella

Noddy and the Broken Bicycle

Noddy and the Cake Contest

Noddy the Champion

Noddy Cheers Up Big-Ears

Noddy Delivers Some Parcels

Noddy and the Difficult Day

Noddy and Father Christmas

Noddy Gets a New Job

Noddy and the Giraffes

Noddy Goes Shopping

Noddy Has an Afternoon Off

Noddy and the Kite

Noddy Lends a Hand

Noddy Loses his Bell

Noddy Loses Sixpence

Noddy the Magician

Noddy and Martha Monkey

Noddy and his Money

Noddy Meets Some Silly Hens

Noddy and the Milkman

Noddy and the Missing Hats

Noddy and his New Friend

Noddy and the Parasol

Noddy and the Pouring Rain

Noddy and the Prize Catch

Noddy and the Special Key

Noddy to the Rescue

Noddy and the Unhappy Car

Noddy and the Useful Rope

Noddy and the Windy Day

Published by BBC Children's Books
a division of BBC Worldwide Publishing
Woodlands, 80 Wood Lane, London W12 0TT
First published 1996
Text copyright © 1996 BBC Children's Books
Stills copyright © 1996 BBC Worldwide
Design copyright © 1996 BBC Children's Books
ISBN 0 563 40541 4

Based on the Television series, produced by Cosgrove Hall Films Limited,
inspired by the Noddy Books which are copyright © Enid Blyton Limited 1949-1968

Enid Blyton's signature and Noddy are trademarks of Enid Blyton Limited

Typeset in 16/22 pt Garamond by BBC Children's Books
Printed and bound in Great Britain by Cambus Litho, East Kilbride
Colour separations by DOT Gradations, Chelmsford
Cover printed by Cambus Litho, East Kilbride